oComelon™

PLAYDATE WITH CODY

Adapted by Tina Gallo

Simon Spotlight

New York London Toronto Sydney New Delhi

SIMON SPOTLIGHT
An imprint of Simon & Schuster Children's Publishing Division
1230 Avenue of the Americas, New York, New York 10020
This Simon Spotlight edition August 2022
CoComelon™ & © 2022 Moonbug Entertainment. All Rights Reserved.
All rights reserved, including the right of reproduction in whole or in part in any form.
SIMON SPOTLIGHT and colophon are registered trademarks of Simon & Schuster, Inc.
For information about special discounts for bulk purchases, please contact Simon & Schuster
Special Sales at 1-866-506-1949 or business@simonandschuster.com.
Manufactured in the United States of America 0722 LAK
10 9 8 7 6 5 4 3 2 1
ISBN 978-1-6659-1885-5
ISBN 978-1-6659-1886-2 (ebook)

JJ is so excited. His best friend, Cody, is coming over for a playdate!

JJ and Cody are so happy to see each other.

Today's our day to play!

Playing with my dinosaur!

Their dads remind them, "When we work together, everyone has more fun!"

Cody chooses to share his dinosaur with JJ.

It's better to work together because it's double the fun!

Next Cody and JJ
decide to color.

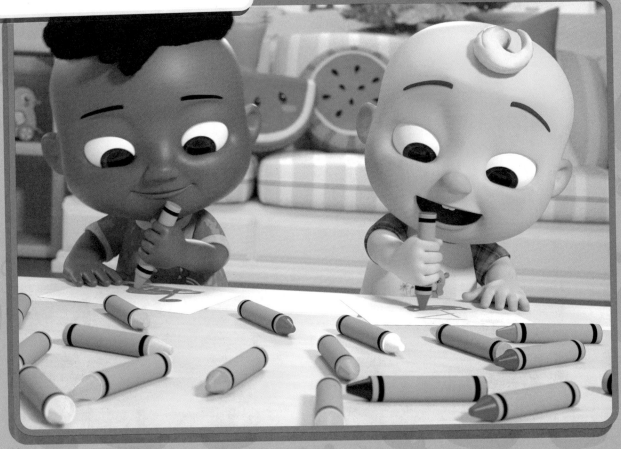

Oh no! Cody and JJ both want the same color crayon.

I want the color dark blue.
Oh no! We just have one.

Cody and JJ take turns using the dark blue crayon.

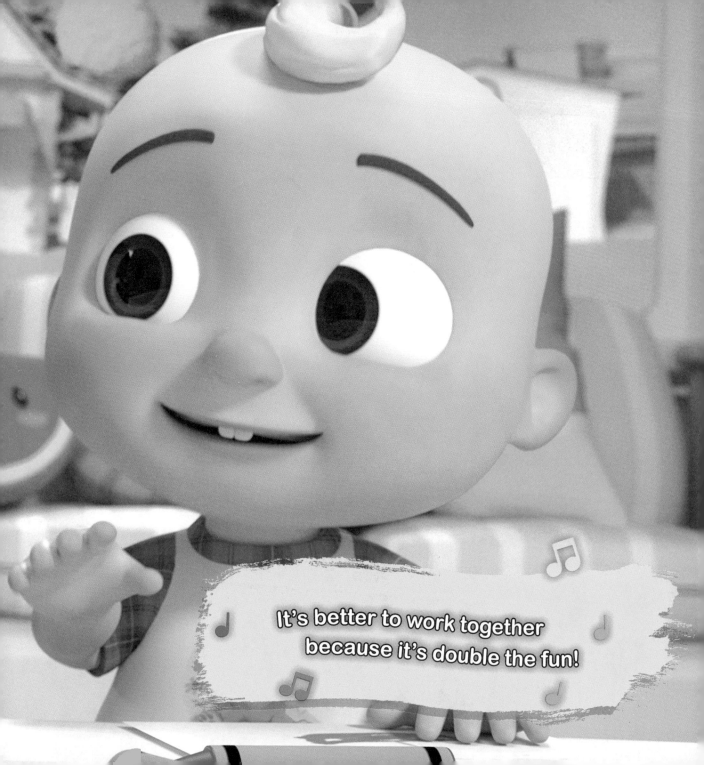

I have fun when you have fun! Yes!
Share when you only have one!

JJ and Cody will ride the tricycle together.

5, 4, 3, 2, 1 . . .

BLAST OFF!

Sharing is fun!